Scholastic Canada Ltd.
604 King Street West, Toronto, Ontario M5V 1E1, Canada

Scholastic Inc.
557 Broadway, New York, NY 10012, USA

Scholastic Australia Pty Limited
PO Box 579, Gosford, NSW 2250, Australia

Scholastic New Zealand Limited
Private Bag 94407, Botany, Manukau 2163, New Zealand

Scholastic Children's Books
Euston House, 24 Eversholt Street, London NW1 1DB, UK

www.scholastic.ca

Library and Archives Canada Cataloguing in Publication
Larry, H. I.
Boot camp / by H.I. Larry ; illustrations by Andy Hook.
(Zac power)
ISBN 978-1-4431-2862-9
I. Hook, Andy II. Title. III. Series: Larry, H. I. Zac Power.
PZ7.L333Bo 2013   j823'.92   C2013-901817-4

Text copyright © 2008 by H.I. Larry.
Illustrations and design copyright © 2008 Hardie Grant Egmont.
All rights reserved.
Published in Australia by Hardie Grant Egmont, 2008.
First Canadian edition published 2014.
Cover and illustrations by Andy Hook.
Based on original illustration and design by Ash Oswald.

6 5 4 3 2 1   Printed in Canada 121   14 15 16 17 18

ZAC POWER™

24 HOURS TO SAVE THE WORLD ... AND ACE A MATH TEST

BOOT CAMP

BY *H. I. LARRY*

ILLUSTRATIONS BY *ANDY HOOK*

Scholastic Canada Ltd.
Toronto New York London Auckland Sydney
Mexico City New Delhi Hong Kong Buenos Aires

CHAPTER... ...ONE

Is there a record for the world's most boring math class? Zac Power wondered to himself. *Because if there is, Ms Tran's about to break it.*

"The square root of a number is the number that is multiplied by itself and gives the first number," his teacher was saying. "For example, 2 is the square root of 4, because 2 times 2 equals 4."

I'll never need to know that, Zac thought. After all, Zac was a spy with GIB (short for the Government Investigation Bureau). At 12, Zac had already aced plenty of tough solo missions, and none of them had had anything to do with square roots.

Zac's whole family worked for GIB, too. His brother Leon wasn't a field agent like the rest of them, though. Leon worked for GIB's Tech Support and Gadget Design Division. He was nice, but definitely a nerd.

Zac yawned loudly.

"Excuse me, Zac Power!" said Ms Tran sternly. "Could you give me an example of a square root?"

Zac thought fast. "Er...3 times 3 equals 9. So, 3 is the square root of 9."

"Good," said Ms Tran, but she didn't smile. "I hope you do as well on the math test tomorrow. Anyone who doesn't get 100% will have to get extra math help after school."

She turned and wrote on the whiteboard.

Math test: 2 p.m. tomorrow

That's so unfair! Zac thought to himself. *I've missed heaps of math classes lately because I've been spying.* But Zac couldn't say that to Ms Tran. His job with GIB was top secret.

With a sigh, Zac checked the clock above Ms Tran's head. *It's 2:05 p.m. now,* he thought. *Only 24 hours until the test.*

"Ms Tran, can I please go to the bathroom?" Zac asked, putting his hand up. He didn't need to go. He just needed a break from math.

Ms Tran nodded. Zac jumped up and headed out of the classroom.

The first thing Zac did when he got to the bathroom was check his hair in the mirror. *It looks perfect,* he told himself. *Extra messy.*

He went into the end stall and sat down on the toilet seat lid. This was where he liked to go when he had SpyPad messages to read, because no one ever came down to the last stall.

I can't get extra math help after school, Zac

thought, feeling worried. *What if GIB needs me for a mission? I have to get 100% on the math test, or my spying career could be ruined.*

Suddenly, Zac felt the floor below the toilet slide sideways under his feet.

WHIRRRR

The next thing Zac knew, his feet were dangling in mid-air! There was a big, black hole where the floor had been.

Zac snapped into spy mode. *Obviously this isn't normal for a toilet,* he thought. *What's going on?*

Holding tightly onto the sides of the toilet, he twisted around for a better look. He could see a thick metal arm coming out of the hole in the ground.

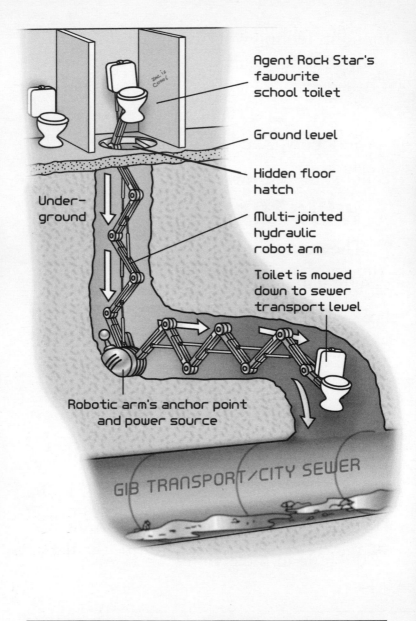

Agent Rock Star's favourite school toilet

Ground level

Hidden floor hatch

Under-ground

Multi-jointed hydraulic robot arm

Toilet is moved down to sewer transport level

Robotic arm's anchor point and power source

GIB TRANSPORT/CITY SEWER

The toilet is mounted on a robotic arm, thought Zac. *Cool!*

Another whirring sound filled the air, and then the toilet beeped like a truck reversing.

BEEP BEEP BEEP!

Zac gripped the sides of the toilet even tighter.

He'd done a lot as a spy, but he'd never ridden a robotic toilet. He guessed it would move pretty fast.

BEEP BEEP BEEP!

A second later, the robotic arm pulled the toilet through the floor!

This is awesome, Zac grinned to himself as the toilet whizzed down into the dark.

Then Zac heard a computerized voice. "Now arriving at the vehicle depot," it said, sounding official.

The robotic toilet slowed down before stopping smoothly.

Zac jumped off the toilet. He was in a dark, musty concrete tunnel. Slimy water dripped on his head.

Gross, he thought. *I must be in a sewer.*

Zac knew that a ride on a robotic toilet could only mean one thing. He had a new mission from GIB. But what did he need to investigate in a smelly sewer?

Then Zac's pocket buzzed. There was a message on his SpyPad, the powerful mini-computer that all GIB spies carried.

CLASSIFIED

FOR THE EYES OF
ZAC POWER ONLY
MESSAGE INITIATED 2:28 P.M.

Congratulations on topping your local spy ladder for 15 weeks in a row. You will now train at GIB Boot Camp against the best GIB spies in the world.

Boot Camp is made up of different training courses, each one based on real-life conditions.

Beware: things at Boot Camp are not always what they seem.

The first spy to complete Boot Camp will be awarded the top position on GIB's Global Spy Ladder.

END

BOOT CAMP
>>> ON

Zac had heard rumours about Boot Camp in spy school. Only the best spies were chosen to go.

Sweet! he thought. *Time off school, and I don't even have to go on a proper mission.*

He just had to make sure he was back in time for the math test. *No worries,* thought Zac. *How hard could Boot Camp be?*

CHAPTER... ...TWO

As Zac's eyes got used to the darkness of the sewer, he noticed a shiny silver vehicle parked nearby.

The vehicle had a pointed nose and a long exhaust-pipe tail. Two red headlights glowed like eyes. Instead of wheels, there were claw-like feet underneath.

It looks like a giant rat! Zac thought.

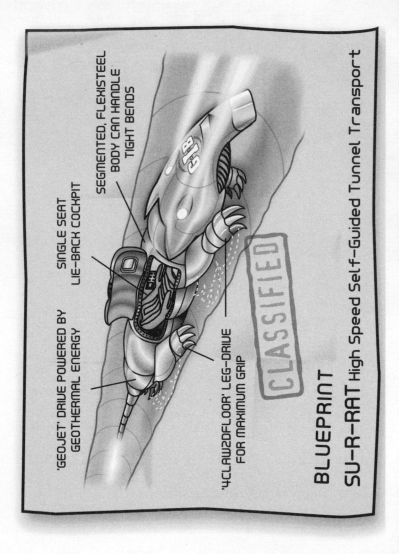

SEGMENTED, FLEXISTEEL
BODY CAN HANDLE
TIGHT BENDS

SINGLE SEAT
LIE-BACK COCKPIT

'GEOJET' DRIVE POWERED BY
GEOTHERMAL ENERGY

'4CLAW2DFLOOR' LEG-DRIVE
FOR MAXIMUM GRIP

CLASSIFIED

BLUEPRINT
SU-R-RAT High Speed Self-Guided Tunnel Transport

Zac lifted the glass hatch and jumped into the cockpit. There was just enough room inside for one.

Zac squinted as a laser beamed straight into his eye. The dashboard screen blinked.

SCANNING...CONFIRMED IDENTITY: AGENT ROCK STAR

An automatic seatbelt snapped tightly over Zac. The roof clamped shut and the engine started whirring.

Then there was a metallic scratching sound, and the SU-R-Rat shot forward. Zac lurched around inside as the vehicle sprinted down the tunnel on its metal legs.

The SU-R-Rat sped through the sewer

for ages, jerking and weaving crazily, until at last it came to a sudden stop.

The roof lifted open, and Zac leaped out. He was in a dark tunnel. Up ahead he could see a metal door in the wall.

BOOT CAMP BRIEFING ROOM AUTHORIZED GIB SPIES ONLY

Before Zac could open the door, a tall, muscly man stepped out of the shadows.

"ATTENTION!" the man barked into Zac's ear.

Zac jumped and spun around. *Who —?*

The man's top lip curled into a snarl. "Are you a spy, or a scaredy-cat?" he screamed.

This guy needs to relax, whoever he is,

thought Zac, standing up straight.

"I am Drill Sergeant Hotsnap!" the man yelled.

Hotsnap was dressed head-to-toe in army greens. His eyes bulged in his sweaty red face.

"I am in charge of Boot Camp! I am not – I repeat, *not* – a nice guy!"

Duh, thought Zac. *You can say that again...*

"Don't just stand there, custard-brain!" screamed Hotsnap.

The metal door swung open. Zac could see a group of spies waiting inside.

"Forward *march*!" Hotsnap ordered.

Zac hated being bossed around. But no one in their right mind would argue with

Hotsnap, so Zac marched briskly into the Briefing Room.

"Left, right, left, right!" bellowed Hotsnap.

The Briefing Room had round walls that were fitted with TV screens that showed what was going on in each training room. In between the TV screens, there were large, round doors.

As Zac marched toward the other spies at the centre of the Briefing Room, his SpyPad buzzed with a new message. It was a map of Boot Camp, downloaded automatically.

Zac quickly flicked the cursor over the map.

There were six different challenge rooms, each joined to the Briefing Room by a long, thin tunnel.

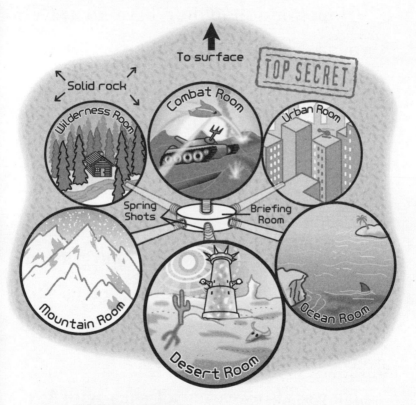

GIB BOOT CAMP
(Underground Elite Spy Training Facility)

The Briefing Room was a bit crowded. Next to Zac, two spies were gossiping. He recognized them both immediately.

"Top spies shouldn't have to travel through sewers," grumbled Agent Pronto, top spy in the Northern Region.

"I suppose it keeps Boot Camp's location secret. Stops enemy agents attacking," said Agent White Crane, best agent in the Far Eastern Region.

Then a third spy leaned over and grinned at them. He looked about twelve, and his hair was cool, all shaggy and streaked green.

He was also wearing a T-shirt with Axe Grinder on it – Zac's favourite band!

Can't believe I'm stuck wearing my school uniform, thought Zac. The SU-R-Rat had messed his hair up badly, and he felt a bit flustered.

"Boot Camp is GIB's highest security

facility," the green-haired spy said. "That's why Commander X's office is here."

Commander X was the head of GIB Global's Undercover Division, a highly secretive part of the agency. Zac knew that X was a master of disguise, and that he was famous for his undercover missions at enemy organizations.

No one even knew what X really looked like.

Agent Pronto looked impressed. "I heard X speaks 12 languages," he said.

"I heard X loves crosswords," added Agent White Crane.

The green-haired spy shrugged and turned away.

Zac watched him curiously.

This new spy looked pretty cool, but Zac had never seen or heard of him before. Zac knew almost all the spies his age at GIB.

Leon had recently installed a brand-new prototype program of the GIB database onto Zac's SpyPad. It helped spies identify friendly agents in the field.

It's a good thing Leon keeps my SpyPad up-to-date with the latest add-ons, Zac thought to himself.

Making sure no one could see him, Zac pointed his SpyPad's scanner toward the new spy. After a moment, a message flashed on the screen.

GIB SPY ID RESULTS: 0

Maybe he's new, thought Zac. But even so, Zac's spy senses were tingling.

I might keep an eye on him anyway. He seems a little too cool to be true.

CHAPTER... ...THREE

"Listen up, knuckleheads!" yelled Hotsnap.

Zac stood at attention. The briefing had begun.

"During Boot Camp, spies will be paired up!" Hotsnap bellowed, glaring at everyone. "You must finish each challenge faster than your opponent! The spy with the fastest overall time is the winner!"

And the winner tops the Global Spy Ladder, Zac finished silently. *If I win, I'll officially be the best spy in the world. Even better than that new green-haired spy.*

Hotsnap grabbed Zac by the shoulder. "Pay attention, princess!" Hotsnap yelled. "Meet 24, your opponent!"

Zac glanced over. He was paired up with the new spy!

"You might be top of your local spy ladder," Hotsnap kept yelling, "but 24 could beat the pants off you!"

As if, Zac thought crossly.

"And don't forget: you must call each other by Boot Camp code numbers!"

Hotsnap threw a pair of dog tags straight

at Zac's head. Zac's code number, 2613, was engraved on the front of the dog tags. There was a small screen to the right.

"2613 and 24!" Hotsnap yelled. "Get to the Desert Room — *now!*"

"Think you're up to this?" 24 said to Zac with a smirk.

Hotsnap had already started yelling at another pair of spies.

Zac scowled. "Let's just find our way to the Desert Room," he said.

"Poor 2613," said 24, shaking his head. "Don't you know that we go by SpringShot?"

24 yanked open one of the doors along the Briefing Room walls. A small sign above the door read "Desert Room."

What a know-it-all, thought Zac as he peered through the doorway. There was a tunnel with padded walls, and at the entrance was a gigantic spring fitted with a pilot seat.

"You can't use gas-powered transport underground because of the fumes," said 24, pushing past Zac. "So GIB came up with SpringShots."

Anyone would think he invented SpringShots, Zac thought, rolling his eyes.

"You just have to sit in the spring," said 24, jumping into the tunnel and settling into the SpringShot seat, "and buckle up!"

The giant spring uncoiled and shot down the tunnel, taking 24 with it. Zac waited, and after a moment, the spring coiled back tight, now empty without 24.

Zac sat in the seat and put the belt on. Then...

SPRRRING!

Strapped into the SpringShot, Zac rocketed deep into the tunnel. Freezing air rushed past as he flew toward the Desert Room. It was like being on a roller coaster!

This is the best part of Boot Camp so far! Zac smiled.

Then Zac spotted a light shining at the end of the tunnel. *How do I stop this thing?* he thought.

Suddenly, the SpringShot stopped and Zac's seatbelt burst open. Like a human cannonball, Zac shot out the end of the spring and hurtled into the Desert Room. He landed upside down on burning hot sand.

"It's called an ejector seat, 2613," 24 smirked. He was standing nearby. "I'm sure you'll get the hang of it."

Zac stood up quickly and brushed himself off, ignoring 24.

The Desert Room was very realistic, and Zac could hardly believe it was underground. Hot electric lights shone down just like the sun, and there were palm trees everywhere. There were also rows of tires dug into the sand, just like an army obstacle course.

The only thing not very desert-like was a huge round tower in the middle. *I guess that's where they watch us,* thought Zac, *to make sure we don't cheat.*

The two spies' dog tag screens crackled to life.

"There are two training bombs hidden in the sand!" Hotsnap bellowed through the screens. "Crawl across the sand on your belly, then find your bomb and disarm it before your opponent disarms theirs!"

Zac sneaked a look over at 24, who winked at him. Zac quickly looked down at his dog tags, feeling slightly worried.

I haven't disarmed a bomb since spy school, he thought. *Not without a gadget, anyway.*

"If you lose, your bomb will explode and bury you in sand!" Hotsnap added. "It will take an hour to dig yourself out!"

An hour! If Zac lost that much time, he'd never beat 24 and win Boot Camp. Plus, he'd miss the math test for sure.

I'll just have to remember how to disarm a bomb, he told himself firmly. *No problem.*

CHAPTER... ...FOUR

Hotsnap's angry face disappeared from the screen, and a message appeared instead.

**BOMB LOCATION FOR AGENT 2613:
GO WEST 441 METRES.
THEN NORTH 169 METRES.
BOMB IS 4 METRES UNDERGROUND.**

441 metres? Zac thought, confused. *That doesn't make sense!*

The desert didn't look that big.

Unless...the directions are in code!

24 pushed past Zac, heading toward the obstacle course.

"I'll wait for you at the finish line, 2613," 24 said slyly. He dropped and crawled on his belly across the sand at top speed.

Has he cracked his own instructions already? Zac wondered, his heart racing. *I'm not going to let him beat me!*

Zac quickly checked the numbers on the dog tag screen again. *Math has been a problem all day*, he thought, remembering Ms Tran's class. *Wait a minute...*

"The square root of a number," Ms Tran had said, "is the number that is multiplied by itself and gives the first number."

Maybe the code is in square roots! That's why the numbers are way too big.

Zac pulled out his SpyPad and switched it to Calculator. *The square root of 441 is 21. So I should go 21 metres, not 441.*

It was only a hunch. But 24 was already way out in front, and Zac decided to trust his instincts.

He dropped onto his belly. As fast as he could, he wriggled 21 metres across the dunes, heading west.

Every so often, he had to struggle under a half-tire. The sand was burning hot, and Zac's arms started to ache.

After 21 metres, Zac stopped and

checked the calculator again. "The square root of 169 metres is 13 metres," he muttered to himself, turning to the right.

He hauled himself across the sand dunes, sweat pouring from him. *I hope 24 hasn't found his bomb already!*

Zac forced himself to crawl faster. At last, he found the spot where the bomb should have been buried.

He checked the code one more time. *Bomb is 4 metres underground,* he thought, calculating quickly, *so I should dig 2 metres.*

Frantically, Zac scooped sand out with his bare hands. The hole got deeper. *Almost there!* Then…

YEEEEEOW!

Shiny black creatures swarmed out of the hole and nipped at Zac's hands.

Scorpions! thought Zac, quickly flicking one off his arm. But the scorpion felt strangely hard and cold.

They're not real scorpions! They're just micro-robots shaped like scorpions.

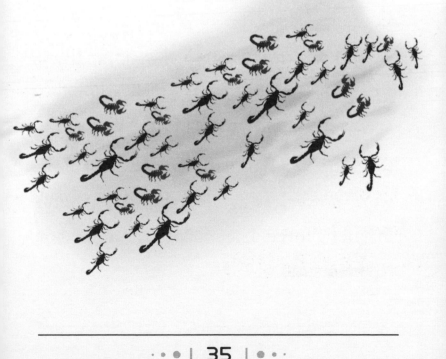

It was a clever trick on GIB's part. They wanted to make the challenge harder.

But Zac had a trick of his own. He happened to be wearing Leon's latest invention, the MagnaBelt.

The buckle was made from a powerful magnet. Leon had only finished it that morning, and wanted Zac to try it on for size before school.

Lucky the belt was cool enough to wear to school, thought Zac, unbuckling it.

He dangled the buckle in the hole in the sand, and the steel robo-scorpions were powerless against the MagnaBelt's magnetic force. The scorpions clamped on to the buckle.

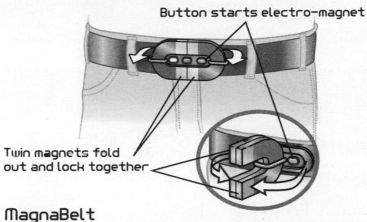

Button starts electro-magnet

Twin magnets fold out and lock together

MagnaBelt
(Concealed Electromagnetic Attractor/Pant Securer)

When all the scorpions were on the buckle, Zac plunged his hand into the sand. He felt around until he touched something at the bottom. *The bomb!* Zac pulled it out and carefully opened it up. The bomb was ticking, getting louder and louder.

TICK! TICK! TICK!

There was a tangle of wires inside, but only one red and one blue wire. Zac knew he had to cut one of those wires to disarm the bomb. *Now which one was it, again?*

Thinking back to spy school, Zac remembered what he'd learned in Emergency Protocol 101.

Red stands for danger, he told himself, *so I should cut the blue wire.*

TICK! TICK! TICK!

Zac grabbed his laser pocket knife and gently picked up the blue wire.

TICK! TICK! TICK!

He took a deep breath and, with a flash of his laser, sliced the blue wire in half.

The bomb stopped ticking right away. Zac had found the bomb and disarmed it perfectly!

I guess school does come in handy, after all, he thought, feeling pleased with himself.

Then Zac turned around to check on his opponent.

He couldn't believe it. 24 was sitting only a few metres away, resting comfortably against a plastic palm tree.

24 had finished the challenge first!

CHAPTER... ...FIVE

How on earth did he beat me? thought Zac furiously.

But before he could say anything to 24, Zac's dog tags buzzed to life.

"Stop all challenges! This is an emergency!" yelled Hotsnap through the screen. "Report to the Briefing Room! This is *not* a drill!"

What's going on? thought Zac. *An emergency at Boot Camp?*

Without another word, Zac and 24 raced toward the tunnel that led back to the Briefing Room. As they ran, Zac caught sight of a pair of gloves tucked into 24's pocket. The gloves had lots of little tears in them.

What does he need gloves for? Zac wondered as he scrambled over the hot sand. The sand was making the little robo-scorpion bites on his arms itch like crazy.

Then Zac realized that 24 didn't have any bites at all. *There would have been robo-scorpions where he was digging, too. He must have known to put gloves on before he started digging.*

But there was no time to ask questions. Zac crawled back into the waiting Spring-Shot and strapped himself in. Then he shot back through the tunnel at top speed.

Zac crash-landed in the Briefing Room and quickly stood at attention in front of Hotsnap. A moment later, 24 flew out of the tunnel and landed gracefully on his feet.

I really don't like him, Zac thought angrily, as 24 stood there smugly. *It's so unfair! I should have won the desert challenge.*

"Listen here, 24 and 2613!" yelled Hotsnap. "Commander X is missing."

Zac stood up even straighter. This was bad news.

"Our intelligence says he was kidnapped from Boot Camp in the last hour. The other spies are already looking for him."

Zac checked his dog tags.

Hotsnap paused for a moment. He didn't look so angry anymore. Now he just looked worried. "It is crucial that we find X as soon as possible. He has Memory Magnets with him, and we know he'll use them to protect GIB."

Magnets can be disguised as coins

Extendable magnetrode arms wipe electric memory fields from wearer's brain

WARNING! EXTREME DANGER

Magnets attach to victim's temples with superstrong glue activated by twisting coin

TOP SECRET:
GIB LAST RESORT MEMORY MAGNETS

Zac stared at Hotsnap in horror.

He knew that Memory Magnets were a complex technology given to high-level GIB spies.

If spies were captured they could stick the Memory Magnets on their foreheads. Their GIB memories would be wiped, one-by-one. This way, the enemy couldn't force them to tell GIB secrets.

The longer X wears the Memory Magnets, thought Zac, *the more memories he'll lose.*

If they didn't find Commander X soon, all of his amazing GIB knowledge would be lost forever and Commander X would never work as a spy again.

I've got to rescue X before he wipes his

memories! Zac thought. *But Boot Camp is huge. Where do I start looking?*

Zac pulled his SpyPad out of his pocket and opened his digital map of Boot Camp.

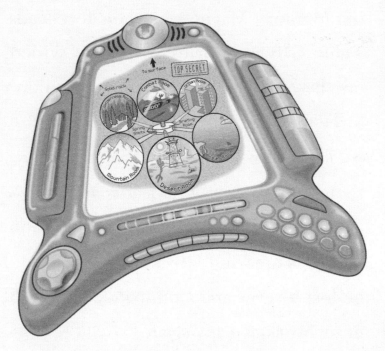

If I were a kidnapper, how would I smuggle X out of Boot Camp? There was only one exit marked on the map, and that was through the Briefing Room.

That seems like a risky way to leave if you're a kidnapper, thought Zac. *There must be another way out of Boot Camp. Wouldn't each room have a fire exit?*

Then it hit him. The Mountain Room had a life-sized mountain.

A fire exit would be near the surface, and you would have to climb the mountain to get out.

Zac felt sure he was onto something. *Maybe the kidnappers smuggled X out through the fire exit?*

"During your search, you must stay together for safety!" Hotsnap was yelling. "Now go!"

Zac groaned. He wanted to search for X by himself!

24 turned to Zac with a smirk. "Where do you want to start, big shot?"

Big shot? thought Zac. *Who says "big shot" these days?*

CHAPTER... ...SIX

"Let's search the Mountain Room first," said Zac casually. "It's as good a place as any to start."

There was something odd about 24, and Zac wanted to keep him at a distance. *I'm not telling him my theory about the fire exit,* he thought firmly.

"Of course, 2613," said 24, rolling his

eyes. "Your spying instincts are superb."

Zac threw 24 a dirty look. "Let's just go."

Zac opened the door to the Mountain Room and buckled into the SpringShot. Seconds later, he was rocketing away from the Briefing Room.

At the end of the tunnel, the ejector seat flung Zac into the air. He landed face-first in a deep pile of cold snow.

Moments later, 24 hurtled through the icy air. He landed smoothly on his feet. "Watch and learn, 2613," said 24 with a wink.

Zac ignored him and looked around, shivering from the cold. They were at the foot of a massive fake mountain. Snow sprinkled down from high above.

Zac knew he needed to get to the top of the mountain to look for a fire exit, and to check for evidence that the kidnappers had been there.

He wiggled his toes. They were nice and toasty in his favourite self-heating sneakers, but the rest of him was freezing! *First, I need to find a snowsuit.*

Nearby, there was a supply hut. Ice axes hung on one wall. Spies needed axes to climb the iciest parts of the mountain. These weren't ordinary ice axes, though. They were fitted with coloured lights and a disco music soundtrack.

Disco ice axes? Zac loved music, but he did wonder why GIB would bother.

A row of high-tech silver snowsuits hung from pegs. Zac and 24 both grabbed suits with "Snowbird" on the label.

As the spies pulled the snowsuits on over their clothes, Zac noticed a dark shape under 24's Axe Grinder T-shirt. It looked like a tattoo!

He's way too young to have a tattoo! thought Zac. *That's one more weird thing about him.*

"What's that on your shoulder?" asked Zac.

"It's, er, just a fake tattoo," 24 said, clearing his throat. His eyes darted from side to side.

The classic sign of a liar, Zac noted. *What is he trying to hide?*

24 quickly pulled on the rest of his

snowsuit, being careful to leave his T-shirt in place.

Snug inside their snowsuits, Zac and 24 began climbing up the mountain. They swung their ice axes into the mountain's icy face.

It was hard work, and very slow going. After an hour, Zac's arms burned with the effort.

They climbed up and up in silence. A few hours went by, and they still had not reached the top.

More than once, Zac doubted whether he was on the right track.

But the Mountain Room seems like the easiest way for the kidnappers to sneak out, he kept telling himself. *And you don't give up on a hunch because it's hard.*

Snow fell into his eyes as he climbed, but Zac kept going. After a while, he started thinking about how much he disliked 24.

For one thing, he's a bit too cool, Zac thought, *but he also says lame things like "big shot." And he's got a tattoo, and it looks real.* Zac didn't know anyone whose parents would let them get a tattoo.

Then he had the weirdest thought. *What if 24's not really a kid?*

Zac shot a glance at 24. He definitely looked like a kid. His face wasn't wrinkled. Plus, he streaked his hair green, which was something a grown-up wouldn't do.

But the evidence isn't much to go on, Zac decided, *so I'll have to test him.*

By now, they'd almost reached the top of the ice wall they were climbing. Beyond the ice wall was a ledge dotted with fake pine trees. It was a perfect spot to rest.

"Break?" Zac called to 24, puffing hard.

24 nodded. They hauled themselves onto the ledge.

Zac checked the time.

"I might listen to some music," Zac said, taking his iPod from his pocket.

He switched the music to Axe Grinder and passed one of the earphones to 24.

"Got your name burned into my brain!" blared the song.

"Like this band?" asked Zac casually.

"They're pretty good," said 24.

Well, you're wearing their T-shirt, Zac thought slyly, setting the iPod to maximum volume. *You're supposed to love them. Most kids do.*

"Is this their third or fourth album?" Zac yelled over the music.

"Fourth!" 24 shrieked back at the top of his voice.

Gotcha! thought Zac. *If you were really into them, you'd know that there are only three Axe Grinder albums! Which means you're probably not a fan, and you're probably not really a kid.*

"You're not…" Zac began.

But his words were cut off by a strange creaking sound.

Suddenly, the world turned white. There was snow everywhere, sliding down the mountain toward them!

Instantly, Zac realized what had happened. 24's shrieking had triggered an avalanche!

Instinctively, Zac sprang into the air and grabbed the branches of a fake pine tree.

The snow roared past underneath his feet as he held on tight.

What's 24 doing? thought Zac.

"Hey, 24!" he yelled, his voice echoing.

But there was no reply.

CHAPTER...
...SEVEN

Zac clung to the fake pine tree for a few more minutes, until he was sure that the avalanche had stopped. The flow of snow seemed to have settled.

Zac jumped down to the ground. *There might be something fishy going on with 24,* Zac thought, *but I can't just leave him to freeze if he's trapped under the snow.*

"24!" Zac called desperately, tramping through the snow. "24, can you hear me?"

Zac kept calling for 24, but there was no reply. Now he'd have to waste time looking for 24. *At least I'm warm,* he thought, wriggling his toes in his toasty sneakers. Then something occurred to him. *Heated sneakers! If I turn them way up, they'll melt the snow.*

But there was so much snow to melt! The plan would only work if Zac could figure out roughly where 24 was buried.

Hang on a minute, Zac thought, listening carefully. *Is that...disco music?*

Zac could hear music coming from his left. He turned and stumbled through the snow toward it. Then he saw a patch of snow that was flashing bright colours.

It's 24's disco ice axe! he thought triumphantly, racing toward the flashing snow. *Now I know why GIB invented such a weird gadget!*

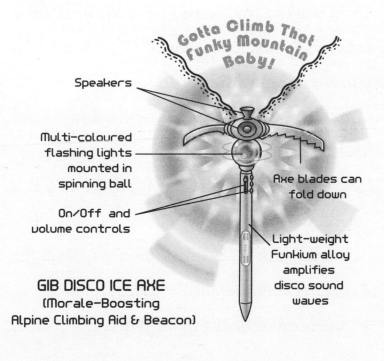

Gotta Climb That Funky Mountain Baby!

Speakers

Multi-coloured flashing lights mounted in spinning ball

Axe blades can fold down

On/Off and volume controls

Light-weight Funkium alloy amplifies disco sound waves

GIB DISCO ICE AXE
(Morale-Boosting Alpine Climbing Aid & Beacon)

Zac shuffled around on the flashing patch of snow, melting it away with his sneakers.

24 was underneath, soaking wet. His snowsuit was battered and torn.

Zac pulled 24 to his feet.

"Thanks a lot, 2613," said 24, breathing heavily. "Next time, maybe warn me when you turn the music up so loud!"

Zac's mouth dropped open. *I just saved his life! What a jerk!*

"Whatever," said Zac furiously. "Let's get on with finding X."

I can't wait to get away from 24, thought Zac. *He's so annoying!*

Pushing this thought from his mind,

Zac looked up. He could see a hole in the roof, and he guessed it was probably the fire exit. There had to be a quicker way to get to the top than by climbing.

But all we've got are ice axes and these stupid itchy snowsuits, he thought, checking the time on his dog tags.

Zac fiddled absent-mindedly with a zipper on his sleeve as he racked his brain. Then something occurred to him.

Why are there zippers on the sleeves of the snowsuit?

He pressed down on the thick, padded arms of his suit.

Wait a minute, he thought excitedly, yanking down the zippers. *These Snowbird suits have mechanical wings sewn into the arms.*

Inside the top layer of his sleeves, there were battery-powered mini-helicopter blades!

If I power up the blades, Zac thought, *I'll reach the fire exit in a second.*

But there was one problem. 24's suit was soaked, and Zac knew the battery would be shot. *I guess I'll just have to take him along for the ride.*

Zac flicked the helicopter blades on his left arm, and then on his right. He held his arms up and out to the side.

Slowly, the helicopter blades unfolded, and then began to spin. They spun faster and faster until Zac's feet lifted off the ground. He was flying!

"What are you doing, 2613?" yelled 24, looking up.

But there wasn't time to explain. As Zac rose higher, he hooked his legs around 24's middle and lifted him into the air.

They flew up toward the roof of the Mountain Simulator. Zac gripped 24 firmly with his legs, but the other spy was struggling against him.

"We're too heavy!" yelled 24. "These mini-helicopters aren't designed to hold two people."

"We'll make it!" Zac yelled back.

But Zac's blades had started to make a whining noise. They were bending under the weight of the two spies.

The fire exit is so close, thought Zac, looking up at the roof. *I can't stop now.* He flicked his blades to Turbo, and hoped that they'd make it.

"Land this instant, 2613!" thundered 24. "That's an order!"

CHAPTER... ...EIGHT

An order? Yeah, right, thought Zac as he strained to reach the fire exit. *24's not my boss!*

Zac's fingertips brushed the concrete exit, and he pulled himself toward it just as the helicopter blades started to slow down. They whined, and smoke started to puff out of Zac's sleeves.

Up close, Zac could see that the exit was easily big enough to smuggle X through. *That's a good start,* he thought.

With a huge effort, Zac pulled himself and 24 up inside the exit just as his blades gave out completely.

The two spies sat there for a moment, breathing heavily.

Then 24 stood up and glared at Zac. "Why are we even up here, 2613?" he spat. "You've got no idea what you're doing! You're the worst spy I've ever met."

Zac forced himself to keep calm. "Let's just keep going," Zac said through gritted teeth. "I have a hunch."

Privately, Zac felt sure he was on the

right track. *I was right about there being an exit,* he thought, *so all I need to do is follow it and I should catch up with X.*

"Whatever," said 24.

Zac ignored 24, and pushed past him down the concrete tunnel, which stretched away from the exit toward the surface.

They trudged along for a hundred metres in silence, until suddenly...

HEE-YAH!

A fully grown man jumped out of nowhere! He ran straight at Zac, karate-chopping wildly. *Maybe he's one of X's kidnappers!* Zac thought, his heart racing.

Zac expertly ducked out of the way of the man's next karate chop.

Then, in the blink of an eye, the man disappeared.

Huh? wondered Zac, breathing heavily. Then he spotted a second man running toward him. The attacker leaped into the air, kicking his legs.

But Zac was too quick. He weaved under the man's legs and dodged him.

Just what I need, Zac thought. *Kidnappers who are also karate pros!*

This time, Zac kept a close eye on his attacker. After a moment, the man flickered and disappeared. It was like a TV set switching off.

Holographic attackers, Zac realized right away. *They must be part of Boot Camp's training system. What an annoying way to get held up.*

"Come on, 24," said Zac, walking faster down the tunnel. "Make sure you don't touch the holograms, because they're probably electrically charged –"

Invisible infra-violet light from 2 projectors creates the 3D Holographic Attacker

50,000 volt electric stun field can knock out an adult agent

Electrified Holographic Attacker

But before Zac could finish his sentence, two more holograms popped up right in front of them. Zac whirled around and ducked their hammering fists.

But 24 wasn't as fast as Zac. Out of the corner of his eye, Zac caught a glimpse of a hologram leaping toward 24!

"Watch out!" Zac yelled, whipping around.

THWACK!

But Zac was too late. The hologram had karate-chopped 24 in the back of the neck!

Sparks flew, and 24 slumped to the ground. Then all the holograms disappeared completely.

24 had blacked out!

CHAPTER... ...NINE

Zac raced over to 24 and shook him carefully. "Wake up, 24," he said loudly. "Wake up!"

Zac tried everything he could think of. He pinched 24, and even gave him his famous cosmic noogie, but nothing worked. 24 was out cold.

Zac checked the time on his dog tags.

I'm running out of time, Zac thought frantically. *X's memories might be being wiped by the minute!*

Then Zac remembered something his gran had once told him.

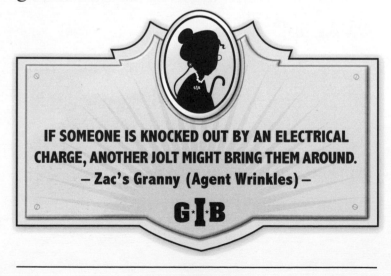

IF SOMEONE IS KNOCKED OUT BY AN ELECTRICAL CHARGE, ANOTHER JOLT MIGHT BRING THEM AROUND.
— Zac's Granny (Agent Wrinkles) —

GIB

It was worth a try. Zac grabbed his SpyPad and carefully lifted off the back cover. There was a tangle of wires inside.

If I put two of them together, they'll make a spark.

Zac rolled up 24's T-shirt, but before he could lay the wires against 24's skin, he gasped.

Up close, 24's tattoo looked real! And it wasn't just any tattoo. *That's a BIG mark!* Zac realized in horror.

BIG was an enemy spy organization. Zac had foiled dozens of evil BIG plans before, but this was really shocking.

An undercover BIG agent in GIB's highest security facility!

If BIG agents are at Boot Camp, they must have kidnapped X! thought Zac. *And if 24's an undercover BIG agent, he must be trying to slow me down. No wonder he didn't want to go up to the fire exit!*

Suddenly, all of the lingering little clues came together.

I'd never seen him before, and he wasn't in the GIB database, Zac told himself. *Plus, I knew he didn't seem like a normal kid. And having a tattoo is especially weird.*

Even 24's awful personality made sense now that Zac knew he was an enemy.

At least Zac had discovered the one

person who could lead him to X. *Now I can make 24 tell me where X is being held.*

He pulled out his iPod headphones and used them to tie up 24's hands. The knot wasn't that secure, but at least it would slow 24 down a bit.

But before Zac could press the SpyPad's wires to 24's skin to jolt him awake, 24 stirred and his eyes fluttered open.

"We're almost there," he murmured. "Almost there."

What is that supposed to mean? Zac wondered. *"Almost there"?*

"24!" Zac said out loud. "Hey, 24, can you hear me?"

24 blinked, and then opened his eyes

properly. He struggled to stand up when he saw Zac.

"You'd better undo these ties, 2613, or you'll regret it," he said furiously, pulling at the ties on his hands.

"I don't think so, 24," Zac replied, hauling him to his feet. "Not if you're a BIG spy. Now, tell me where they've taken X!"

"Never," 24 said, smiling nastily.

CHAPTER... ...TEN

"Suit yourself," said Zac, giving him a firm push in the back. "You'll just have to come with me while I look for X, then."

24 muttered angrily as he shuffled along, his hands still tied together. "Where are we going now?" 24 spat. "You've got no idea what you're doing."

Actually, thought Zac, *I think I'm closer*

than ever. *Didn't he say before that we're "almost there"?*

They moved down the pipe until they came to a metal ladder bolted to the wall. Looking up, Zac saw a patch of light. The surface!

Zac loosened 24's binds so that he could climb the ladder, and made him go up first. Then Zac followed, keeping a close watch.

When they'd climbed out of the tunnel, they found themselves completely surrounded by a thick forest.

Directly in front of them was a log cabin. But the shutters were closed, and the lights were off.

It doesn't look like anyone's there, Zac thought, feeling confused. *Why would the kidnappers be sitting in the dark?*

Suddenly, a strange noise pierced the silence.

AR-ROOOOOOO!

Zac whipped around. There were three wolves advancing toward them! Spit dripped from their shining fangs as they started to growl.

Thinking fast, Zac flicked his SpyPad to Camera. He pointed it at the wolves, and the flash popped in their eyes.

The wolves howled. They were blinded, but only for a moment. Not wasting any time, Zac dragged 24 into the cabin and slammed the door behind him.

What now? he thought, looking around. He could hear the wolves scratching at the front door. He glanced at his dog tags.

The cabin was small and cozy, with a comfy-looking couch next to the fireplace, and a little kitchen off to one side. Zac's sharp eyes spotted a crossword book open on the table.

X loves crosswords, Zac remembered. *But*

if this is his book, why is it in a deserted log cabin in the middle of the forest?

Zac glanced at the puzzle. 24 down was already filled in.

DOWN clues (cont'd.)
24 A false impression of reality.
umber that, multiplied
the

The hairs on the back of Zac's neck stood up. *Is this a clue?*

24 wasn't paying any attention to Zac. Instead, he was looking out of the window at the wolves.

The wolves weren't growling or scratching at the door anymore. They were pawing the glass and wagging their tails at 24.

24 caught Zac staring at him, and he quickly shuffled away from the window toward the couch.

The wolves were acting like 24's pet dogs, thought Zac. *How weird...*

Then a radical thought popped into Zac's mind.

The crossword book made sense if the cabin was X's house. The friendly wolves and 24 murmuring that they were "almost there" made sense as well, if…

24 and X are the same person! thought Zac excitedly. He turned to face 24, who was sitting calmly on the couch.

Evidence slotted together in Zac's mind. *Even the Boot Camp code names are a clue,* he realized slowly. *X is the 24th letter of the alphabet, so X equals 24.*

Zac's code name was 2613, because because Z is the 26th letter of the alphabet, A is the first and C is the third.

And if X is a master of disguise, Zac thought finally, *that explains X's enemy tattoo.* He'd been forced to get it to go undercover with BIG.

Zac looked straight at 24 and said, "I get it. You're Commander X!"

For a long time, 24 looked at Zac. Then he grabbed his hair by the green streak and yanked.

24's whole face peeled off. It was only a high-tech latex mask.

Underneath the mask was a totally different face. It belonged to a much older man. It was Commander X.

"If you're here," Zac said slowly, "then why did you fake your own kidnapping?"

He realized that the crossword had been a clue to tell him that the kidnapping was an "illusion."

"You should know something, Agent Rock Star," said Commander X in a deep, calm voice. 24's unfriendly tone was gone.

"You have great potential, and I hope you'll lead GIB one day. I faked my own kidnapping to test you. It was one of many tests you must pass."

For once, Zac was speechless. Then he remembered the mini-helicopter blades, and 24 ordering him to land.

It was really X ordering me, he thought guiltily. *He slipped out of character because I was putting us both in danger.*

"While the other spies completed Boot Camp," Commander X continued, "you and I went on our own mission. I wanted to see how you'd handle competition from a direct rival like 24."

Zac remembered how annoying and

sarcastic 24 had been. Zac had even worried that 24 might be a better spy.

"24 made you doubt yourself," X said, "but you kept going and completed the mission anyway. That tells me you are a great spy and future leader."

Zac flushed red with pride. This was amazing!

"Preparing to lead GIB Global takes years of hard work," X went on. "There will be regular missions as well as extra training. That's why you need to start while you're young."

Zac nodded. *Whatever it takes, I'll do it,* he thought proudly.

"Never tell anyone what I have told you

today," Commander X finished. "Are you prepared to do this?"

I'm used to hiding the fact that I'm a spy from everyone anyway, Zac thought.

"Definitely!" he said firmly.

Commander X smiled warmly. "I know you'll do really well, Agent Rock Star."

Zac nodded again, and then checked his dog tags one last time.

If he went home via SU-R-Rat, he'd easily make it back to school in time for the math test. But there'd been no time to study. He needed to get 100%, or else he'd have to get extra help!

Going for extra math help would definitely interfere with GIB's big plans for me! Zac thought.

But Commander X seemed to know what Zac was thinking. "I was particularly impressed," he said slyly, "with your code-breaking skills in the Desert Simulator. Nice work on the square roots!"

Zac grinned at him. *I'd forgotten about that,* he thought. *Maybe I can ace this math test after all!*

...**THE END**...